YVONNE IVINSON

THREE IMPORTANT JOBS

Greenwillow Books
An Imprint of HarperCollinsPublishers

To Ottilie

Library of Congress Cataloging-in-Publication Data is available.
ISBN 978-0-06-284291-6 (hardback)
23 24 25 26 27 RTLO 10 9 8 7 6 5 4 3 2 1
First Edition
Greenwillow Books

Wolf Cub had three important jobs to do. She had
no time to listen to the birds or sniff the morning dew.
She had to be fast and focused. Big Wolf needed her
help, and she was determined to do her very best.

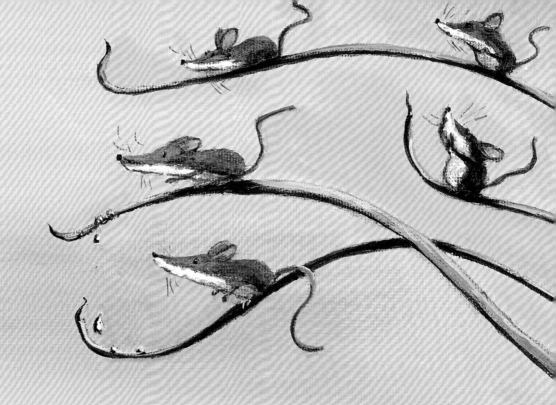

Wolf Cub crept through the tall
meadow grasses. SNAP! She grabbed
Little Mouse in her jaws.

"Oh, dear!" said the other mice. "Poor
Little Mouse!"

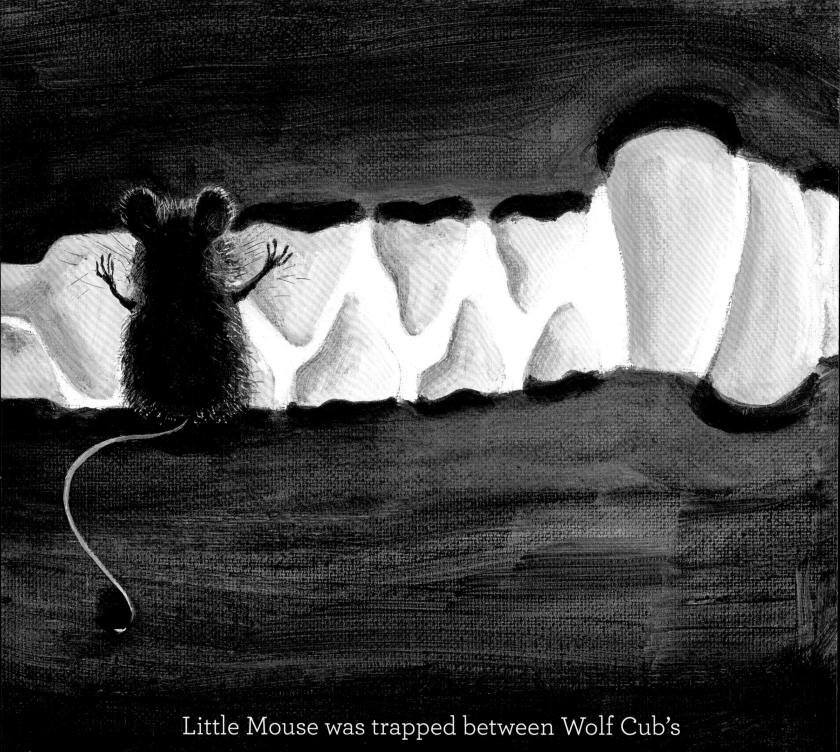

Little Mouse was trapped between Wolf Cub's strong, sharp teeth. She tapped and scratched her tiny claws on Wolf Cub's magnificent molars. "Let me out!" she shouted.

But Wolf Cub didn't answer. She had to keep her mouth firmly closed, so Little Mouse wouldn't escape.

Little Mouse tickled Wolf Cub's tongue with her whiskers.

"Ha-ha! Hee-hee!" Wolf Cub tried to stop giggling. It was impossible.

When Wolf Cub reached the den, Big Wolf
clapped her paws with joy. "Well done,
Wolf Cub!" she exclaimed. "You found
Little Mouse and brought her to me.
You are such a good wolf cub!"

Wolf Cub gently dropped Little Mouse into Big Wolf's paw.

Little Mouse had never seen such a huge wolf with such huge, sharp teeth. "Oh, please don't eat me, Big Wolf!" she cried. "I'm just a mouse!"

"I promise you won't feel a thing, my friend,"
said Big Wolf. "Please close your eyes and we'll go
into my lovely den...."

Meanwhile, Wolf Cub was racing through the forest, on her way to her second important job. She was heading to the sunny hill where the rabbits lived.

Wolf Cub knew exactly where Floppy Rabbit was playing. SNAP! She lifted him right off the ground.
"Oh, dear," said the other rabbits. "Poor Floppy Rabbit!"

Floppy Rabbit was sandwiched between Wolf Cub's fierce, pointy teeth. He smacked his long ears against Wolf Cub's splendid canines. "Let me out!" he shouted.

But Wolf Cub didn't answer. She had to keep her mouth firmly closed, so Floppy Rabbit wouldn't escape.

Floppy Rabbit tickled Wolf Cub's gums with his soft, rabbity furriness.

"Ha-ha! Hee-hee!" Wolf Cub tried to stop giggling. It was impossible.

When Wolf Cub reached the den, Big Wolf threw her paws into the air. "Good job, Wolf Cub!" she exclaimed. "You found Floppy Rabbit and brought him to me. You really are a very good wolf cub indeed."

Wolf Cub carefully placed Floppy Rabbit onto
Big Wolf's paw. Floppy Rabbit had never been so close
to such a huge wolf with such enormous teeth.

"Oh, please don't eat me, Big Wolf!" cried Floppy Rabbit.
"I'm just a rabbit!"

"I promise you won't feel a thing, my friend,"
said Big Wolf. "Please close your eyes and we'll
go into my lovely den...."

Meanwhile, Wolf Cub had one last
job to do. She had to fetch a sack of soft
prickle brushes from Mrs. Hedgehog.
She crept through the thorny hedge,
careful not to wake the sleeping hoglets
and make them grumpy.

When Wolf Cub got back to the den, she gingerly
delivered the sack of prickle brushes to Big Wolf.
"Wonderful, Wolf Cub!" exclaimed Big Wolf.
"You've brought me the brushes. What an excellent
wolf cub you are!"

Big Wolf rubbed her huge paws together. "Thank you, Wolf Cub. You've been very helpful. And now it's your turn to come inside and sit in my lovely den . . .

"—tist's chair to have your teeth cleaned, too!"

"We promise you won't feel a thing," said Little Mouse.

"Not a thing," said Floppy Rabbit.

So Wolf Cub jumped up onto the special chair
and opened her mouth as wide as wide could be.
"Aha!" said Big Wolf. "Your teeth are beautiful!"

Wolf Cub, Fluffy Rabbit, and Little Mouse each got
one of Mrs. Hedgehog's soft brushes.
  Then Wolf Cub showed her new friends how to brush
up, down, and all around.

"Oh, that tickles me," said Little Mouse.

"Me, too," said Floppy Rabbit.

"Ha-ha! Hee-hee!" Wolf Cub tried to stop giggling.

It was impossible.

Wolf Cub beamed at Big Wolf with squeaky-clean teeth. Helping Big Wolf was the best job of all, but being fast and focused had made Wolf Cub suddenly very sleepy. Sweet dreams, Wolf Cub!